THE MAGICAL WORLD OF LUCY-ANNE

Written by
DEREK SMITH

Illustrated by
TONY KENYON

WALKER BOOKS
AND SUBSIDIARIES
LONDON • BOSTON • SYDNEY

To Woodgrange Elfins,
who especially like stories

First published 1995 by Walker Books Ltd
87 Vauxhall Walk, London SE11 5HJ

This edition published 1996

2 4 6 8 10 9 7 5 3 1

Text © 1995 Derek Smith
Illustrations © 1995 Tony Kenyon

This book has been typeset in Plantin Light.

Printed in England

British Library Cataloguing in Publication Data
A catalogue record for this book is available
from the British Library.

ISBN 0-7445-4746-6

CONTENTS

"What are you doing in my garden?"
said Lucy-Anne.

Lucy-Anne
and the Elephant

Lucy-Anne got up and went out into the garden. At the bottom of the garden she could see a large grey blanket hanging on the line. As she went closer she could see it was a peculiar blanket. It had an eye and it wasn't on the line. It had four thick, sturdy legs, and a trunk and tusks.

It was an elephant.

"What are you doing in my garden?" said Lucy-Anne.

"It's my garden," said the elephant.

"No it isn't," said Lucy-Anne. "That's my house." And she pointed to the house.

"Do you live in the garden?" said the elephant.

"Of course not," said Lucy-Anne.

"Well, I do," said the elephant. "So you have the house, I don't mind that, and I'll have the garden. That's fair, isn't it?"

"What about my swing? It's not strong enough for you."

"If I break *my* swing, that's *my* problem. Anyway, I'm hungry." And he began to eat the lupins.

"Hey! You can't eat those!"

"Why not?" He ate some more, but: "Oooaagh! Why didn't you tell me they tasted dreadful?"

"Because I didn't know," said Lucy-Anne. "Now, I think it's time you left."

"Isn't there anything to eat in this garden?" said the elephant. "Flowers, flowers and more flowers. I can't live on those."

"We didn't know you were coming."

The elephant grew angry and charged round, knocking down the washing-line, the swing and the shed.

"Stop it, stop it, stop it!" shouted Lucy-Anne. "Haven't you any manners?"

"I'm hungry," said the elephant.

"If you sit down, I'll fetch you some food, but please get off the rose bed."

The elephant got off.

"Now, behave yourself and I'll see what I can find." Lucy-Anne went into the house.

She came back a few minutes later with a slice of bread and a bottle of lemonade.

"Is that all?" exclaimed the elephant.

"Yes," said Lucy-Anne. "And if you don't want it..."

"I'll have it," he said quickly.

She gave him the bread and poured the lemonade into his mouth.

"That's a bit better," said the elephant.

"I do get bad-tempered when I haven't eaten."

For the first time that morning Lucy-Anne looked about her. In all the surrounding gardens were animals. She saw a giraffe eating an apple tree, a hippopotamus in a goldfish pond, a bison caught in a washing-line, a kangaroo stuck up a walnut tree, a lion on a roof and a gorilla hanging from a TV aerial. Then her daddy came out into the garden.

"My heaven, what's going on!"

"I'm awfully sorry," said the elephant. "I'll pay for the damage."

"How?" said Daddy.

"I'll work for you," said the elephant. "D'you want any logs pulled?"

"No," said Daddy.

"D'you want any loads carried?"

"No," said Daddy.

"D'you want a wall charged down?"

"No," said Daddy.

The elephant scratched his head with his trunk.

"He was hungry," said Lucy-Anne.

"That's no excuse," said Daddy.

Suddenly there was a siren-like call. Lucy-Anne looked and saw it had been made by the gorilla.

"Time to go," said the elephant.

"Where?" said Lucy-Anne.

"To another street," said the elephant. "This one's useless."

"What's wrong with it?" said Daddy.

"No grub," said the elephant, turning towards the house.

"How will you get to the street?" asked Daddy.

"Through the hall," said the elephant, "of course."

11

"But it's too narrow..."

The elephant climbed the back steps, which were metal but only buckled a bit. He drew in a breath and squeezed through the open door. Huffing and puffing, he forced his way down the passage.

"Mind the mirror!" shouted Lucy-Anne.

"Watch the coat hooks!" yelled Daddy.

"Light bulb coming!" shouted Lucy-Anne.

"Light bulb gone," sighed Daddy.

The elephant was now at the end of the hallway and had stopped.

"The front door is closed!"

"Yes?"

"Open it!"

"We can't get to it," said Daddy. "You're in the way. You'll have to back out."

There was a silence and then: "I'm stuck!"

Daddy threw up his hands in dismay.

Lucy-Anne peered down the hallway thoughtfully.

"I think I can get over the top," she said.

"Watch out for broken light bulb," said Daddy.

Lucy-Anne went in as far as the elephant's rump. She took hold of his tail.

"I'm going to climb over," she said. "All right?"

"Do what you have to," he answered, "but no tickling."

She used the tail like a rope and was able to pull herself on to his back. There wasn't much room between it and the ceiling, and she bumped her head. But she managed to wriggle forward.

"I said no tickling," chuckled the elephant.

"Sorry," said Lucy-Anne. He was chuckling and shaking so much, she almost slipped off. But at last she reached his head.

At last Lucy-Anne reached the elephant's head.

Peeping over the top, she saw that his trunk led all the way down to the doormat.

"Here I go!" she exclaimed and pushed herself off.

She went down the trunk head first, just the way she liked to do on the playground slide.

"Well done," said the elephant.

Lucy-Anne fiddled with the latch and opened the door.

"You'll need some help with the last bit," she said. "I'll give you a pull."

"And I'll push," called Daddy.

There followed a grunting and a heaving. A big bit of plaster fell down off the wall.

But suddenly the elephant came free like a cork from a bottle, with Daddy right behind. Lucy-Anne fell over backwards and Daddy fell on top of her. The elephant stood close by, flapping his ears to get rid of the plaster dust.

"Thanks for the push," he puffed at last.

"Good exercise," said Daddy.

"And thanks for the pull," he said to Lucy-Anne. "And for breakfast as well."

Her reply was drowned out by a second siren call from the gorilla. The elephant looked at her sadly.

"I hate goodbyes," he said, all of a sudden. "Do come and see me when we're fixed up."

"Love to." She smiled.

The elephant curled his trunk round her middle and carried her on to the pavement, where all the other animals were gathered. He put her down gently and went to stand next to a zebra. The gorilla did a quick count and then waved to Lucy-Anne and Daddy.

"Thanks for your help!" he called out.

Daddy nodded, thinking about the

damage. But Lucy-Anne called back, "It was a pleasure!"

As the group marched away down the street, they sang, "For she's a jolly good fellow!"

And Lucy-Anne smiled and thought to herself that they were jolly good animals.

There were a few other people already there.

LUCY-ANNE
AND THE BUS RIDE

"I'm afraid we've got a boring ride today,"
said Daddy to Lucy-Anne as they walked to
the bus stop.

There were a few other people already
there: a fat woman with a shopping bag, a
thin man with very long arms and a cowboy
in a tasselly leather jacket.

"Have you been waiting long?" said
Daddy.

"Twelve minutes," said the cowboy, who
was carrying a guitar case. "I'll be late for
the country-and-western show."

"Disgraceful, these buses," said the fat
woman. "They don't come and then they

come six at a time."

"They can't not come and then come six at a time," said Lucy-Anne.

"Oh, they do, they do," said the fat woman. "I assure you, they do."

Daddy said, "It's so boring, standing waiting," and just as he finished a yawn, the bus came round the corner.

The fat woman got on first.

"About time," she said to the driver as she paid her fare.

"Traffic," said the driver. "Terrible this morning."

"It says every ten minutes on the time-table," said the fat woman.

"I got here as fast as I could."

Lucy-Anne and her daddy got on and paid their fares.

"I just hope we don't crawl along," grumbled Daddy as they went to their seats.

The bus started. Lucy-Anne had brought a colouring-book and some pens, but she found it very hard to colour with the bus moving. She said to her daddy, "This page is going to be a bit messy." But he was reading his newspaper.

I wish I had brought my storybook, she thought. Or my French knitting.

Just then the bus lurched and Lucy-Anne was thrown back in her seat.

"What's going on?" said Daddy.

"Please don't panic!" It was the driver's voice, coming from a loudspeaker.

"And why should we panic?" said the fat woman.

"I'm afraid we have just taken off," said the driver, "but I am doing my best to get matters under control."

All the passengers looked out. The bus was high in the air and rising.

It began to roll like a ship at sea.

"Now lookee here," said the cowboy. "We must balance this bus. All you guys and gals with names beginning with a letter between 'A' and 'K' sit on this side. Everyone else on the other."

"I demand to know why we are flying," said the fat woman.

"Yes," said the thin man. "Me too."

"It's never happened before," said the driver. "Not in the twenty-five years I've had this job."

"If I wanted to fly I would have gone to an airport," said the fat woman.

"Me too," said the thin man again.

The cowboy was standing up in the aisle.

"Let's have some organization," he called. "Is anyone in this outfit an aeroplane pilot?" Nobody was. "Now ain't that a shame," he said.

Lucy-Anne was gazing down out of the window. How small everything looked! Tiny cars, houses like doll's houses, and all about the bus seagulls swirled. They made Lucy-Anne feel quite giddy. Then everything became misty.

"We're in a cloud," said the driver. "Somewhere over Hampstead Heath, or it might be Finsbury Park."

"Hackney Marshes," said the cowboy.

"Then we are quite off our route," said the driver.

"I've got a hospital appointment," said the fat woman.

"Me too," said the thin man.

"I'm the lead singer of my band," said the cowboy. "They can't start without me."

Lucy-Anne looked at him with new eyes. She hadn't realized he was quite so important.

The driver was shaking his head and muttering, "Twenty-five years! Twenty-five years on the buses! But never in all that time..."

"I shall write to my member of parliament," declared the fat woman. "I shall write to my councillor, I shall write to the bus company."

"Me too," said the thin man.

"In fact I shall start a petition at once." She got out a sheet of paper from her bag and wrote, *We, the undersigned, declare it a dreadful disgrace that we should be in a flying bus, and we demand to be put down immediately.*

"I wouldn't demand that," said Lucy-Anne. "I think it would be safer if we landed quite slowly."

"I am just saying 'immediately'," said the fat woman, "so they'll get a move on. Now, who wants to sign?"

"Me," said the thin man.

Meanwhile, the cowboy was searching about the bus, scratching his chin. "Something is keeping us up in the air," he said. "Otherwise we'd fall down."

"Good thinking," said the thin man.

"And I think it's that," said the cowboy, pointing to the roof.

They all looked up, and above them was an oblong of sky. Two flaps, like double doors, were open and Lucy-Anne could just see them outside, extended like wings.

"I didn't realize they'd come open," said the driver. "They haven't been open in..."

"Twenty-five years?" said Lucy-Anne helpfully.

"Yes," said the driver.

"Right," said the cowboy. "We must close them."

Everyone looked at each other and nodded wisely.

"Please don't close them too quickly," said the fat woman.

"But I thought you wanted to land immediately," said Lucy-Anne.

"I've changed my mind," said the fat woman and she tore up her petition. "It doesn't matter if I'm late for the hospital."

The bus had come out of the cloud into bright sunlight.

"There's Tower Bridge!" said Lucy-Anne. "And the Tower of London!"

Below them the river Thames glinted like silver.

"So all we need now," said the cowboy, "is one of us to go up on the roof."

"I can't," said the fat woman. "My arthritis."

"Mine too," said the thin man.

Lucy-Anne said, "I'll go."

"Jolly good," said the fat woman.

"Mighty fine," said the cowboy.

"Remember to hold on tight," warned Daddy. "And don't lose your scarf."

Then the thin man lifted her up with his long arms and put her through the oblong hole.

The wind hit her at once. Her coat fluttered out behind like a flag. She settled herself on her knees and put one hand under each of the two flaps. They were icy cold. She began to close them.

"Not so fast!" yelled the driver, as the bus made a dive towards the ground.

Lucy-Anne eased the flaps back a little and the dive became gentler.

"That's better," shouted the cowboy.

It was hard, cold work for Lucy-Anne. But once the flaps were closed a bit, she found she could use her feet and her knees to help. That made it easier. And at last the bus landed on the road.

Lucy-Anne carefully reopened one flap and slipped back in, closing the flap tight behind her.

The warmth of the inside of the bus was like a hot bath. Still, Daddy rubbed her hands in his, to take the chill off.

"That was a good job well done," called the driver. "Now, let's get going! We're not too badly off course, after all!"

Everybody straightened themselves up and settled back into their seats – and in not many minutes the bus pulled up at the hospital stop.

The fat woman was delighted. "I shall be *early* for my appointment!"

So was the thin man.

And so was the cowboy. When they

reached his stop, he said, "I've got *lots* of time before my show."

"Ah," said the driver. "It's quicker by air."

"It was certainly interesting," said Daddy. "But I hope it won't happen again for a while."

Lucy-Anne gave a secret smile as they got off the bus at their stop. She hoped it might happen again quite soon.

Every day, Lucy-Anne came out to see how much taller the plants had grown.

LUCY-ANNE
AND THE RUNNER-BEAN TENT

One day in spring, Lucy-Anne showed her daddy a picture in a book she was reading.

"Can we have a runner-bean tent, Daddy?"

Daddy looked at the picture. "I don't see why not."

So he dug a patch of ground and in the middle put a tall bamboo pole. Then he tied some strings to the top and pegged them in the ground in the shape of a tent. Then Lucy-Anne and he planted a bean by each peg and they watered them every day.

In a few weeks, the runner beans came out of the ground with their first leaves. In the next few weeks, they began to twine round the strings and climb up. The leaves were heart-shaped and bigger than Lucy-Anne's hands. Every day, she came out to see how much taller the plants had grown.

One day she came to see and the plants had stopped growing. She was sure of it, but just to check she tied a piece of cotton to the string where one of the plants had reached. Next day she saw that the plant had definitely grown no higher. Nor had it the next.

"There's something wrong," said Daddy, scratching his head. "I wish I knew what."

The leaves were going floppy, even though he and Lucy-Anne were careful never to let the earth go dry.

"This has got me beat," said Daddy, going into the house to read his gardening books.

Lucy-Anne walked around the bean

plants, examining them closely. She held a limp leaf in her hand.

"This is a very sad plant," she said – and no sooner had she spoken than – *whoosh!* – she found she'd turned into a bean!

She was lying on top of the soil. It took her a little time to get over the surprise. Far above, she could see the beanpole and the wilting plants twined round the strings. Even the grass at the edge of the lawn looked high from where she lay.

Well, she thought, I can't move at all. It's just as well the sun is shining.

A chaffinch flew down. It pecked about in the soil for a bit before it spotted her. It rolled her over and picked her up in its beak. But luckily she was too big for it, so it dropped her. She bumped back on to the soil.

A little later, Daddy came out. He was

carrying a watering-can, but first of all he just stood and looked.

"A bean!" he exclaimed, getting down to soil level. "I wonder how that got here. It hasn't sprouted. It must be a dud."

He was going to kick Lucy-Anne away, but then noticed this was a very handsome bean, fat and shiny, the black speckles on the purple making a most unusual pattern.

"That speckle looks like an eye," he said with a laugh. "You deserve a chance." He poked a hole in the soil with his thumb. He dropped Lucy-Anne in and covered her up.

What Daddy did next, she had no idea. The damp soil was heavy on her. It was like being trodden on. The darkness was heavy, too, like a thick curtain dropped over her. It was quite unpleasant.

Something long and pink wriggled by. She wanted to ask its advice, but it was gone before she could introduce herself.

Lucy-Anne felt water seeping into her through her bean-skin. She felt her bean-self puffing up.

If this goes on I will pop, she thought.

But she didn't pop – she split.

She felt better. It was like taking off a pair of tight shoes. But—

Oh, I must find some light! she thought and sent out a little shoot to explore. At the same time she sent out a root because all beans need roots.

Her shoot pushed up between lumps of soil and stones. After a while Lucy-Anne felt weak with the effort. But she knew she *had* to find light...

And then she did! Her shoot pushed past one last stone and she was above ground.

At first the sunshine was dazzling and she could see nothing but bright white. And then, in a wondrous minute, colour flowed into things: the colours of flowers, of green grass and leaves, and the blue of the sky. She felt so alive, she wanted to eat the light.

Oh, wonderful sun, thought Lucy-Anne, *I will grow up to you.* And she stretched, and her two new leaves reached up like fingers. They touched a string and she knew what she had to do.

Twisting about like a corkscrew, she curled round the string, growing upwards and putting out more leaves.

A couple of black fly landed on one of her leaves. She felt them nibble. But she was in luck, for a six-spot ladybird landed on the leaf and ate the flies. Lucy-Anne was sorry she had no more to offer the ladybird, as it was beautiful and she wanted it to stay. But it spread its wings and flew off.

And then she began to feel an ache in her

roots. At first it was like sore feet. She tried to ignore it. But soon it got so bad, she found she could think about nothing else. She even stopped growing.

Wearily looking about her, she found she had reached the same height as the other bean plants. Her leaves began curling, like theirs, and her stem went flabby. The sun dried her out and made her too hot.

It was just as well she became a girl again.

Lucy-Anne was standing there, on her own two feet, with her own arms, her own head and body, looking down at a hole in the soil. Her hands were her own hands, not leaves.

She saw Daddy by the shed, stretched out in a deckchair. She went over and said, "I know what's wrong with the beans."

He looked up in surprise. "What?"

"They've got root problems," she said.

Daddy rubbed his chin thoughtfully. "You could be right, you know."

"I am."

Daddy laughed, then got up and went into the shed, saying, "Liquid phosphate." Lucy-Anne could see him searching about. He always had difficulty finding things in the shed.

At last he came out with a large plastic bottle.

"Plant food for the roots," he said.

He poured a little into a watering-can, which he then filled with water from the tap. He sprinkled the mixture over the ground where the runner beans were.

He said, "We'll know by tomorrow."

The next day, the plants did look happier. The leaves weren't curling and the stems were stronger. He repeated the treatment daily, and pretty soon the plants were growing again and looking well. Daddy said Lucy-Anne had saved them.

During June, scarlet flowers came and in July, as they faded, little bean pods began to grow. The heart-shaped leaves were so big and so many, you could barely see anything through them.

One hot day, Lucy-Anne wanted somewhere cool to sit and thought, I'll go in the runner-bean tent.

She pulled aside the leaves at the bottom, crawled in and sat down. She put her legs round the pole and looked up. Glints of light came through the green.

She thought, This is too nice for just me, so she crawled out of the tent again and fetched from her bedroom an armful of dolls and stuffed toy animals. She arranged them in a circle in the shade of the leafy tent, and gave them tea.

"I shall come here all summer long."

Lucy-Anne felt happy, not just for herself and her dolls and animals, but for the bean plants with their strong, healthy roots.

Daddy looked in and said, "That's the best tea party I've ever seen."

"I shall come here all summer long," said Lucy-Anne as she refilled the cups.

A bite-shaped piece of toast came away from the rest.

INVISIBLE LUCY-ANNE

Lucy-Anne came into the kitchen, where her daddy was reading a newspaper.

"Look at me," she said.

"Why?" said her daddy without looking up.

"Because I've turned invisible."

Then her daddy did look and saw she wasn't to be seen.

"Do you think it's serious?" said Lucy-Anne.

"Depends," he said, watching as hard as he could where her voice was coming from, in the hope of catching sight of her. But not even her clothes showed up.

"I only noticed," she said, "when I saw my toothbrush, in the bathroom mirror, brushing by itself."

"Have some breakfast," said Daddy. "And perhaps it'll go away."

Lucy-Anne picked up a slice of toast and began to eat. Her daddy stared as the slice rose into the air. He saw a bite-shaped piece come away from the rest and mash itself up. Then he saw it travelling slowly downwards until it disappeared.

"Please don't stare," said Lucy-Anne, taking a drink of juice.

Her daddy tried not to stare at the glass in mid-air pouring itself out and the juice disappearing just as the toast had done.

He shook his head. "You can't go to school like that."

"Why not?" said Lucy-Anne, rolling a marble backwards and forwards on the table.

Daddy's hand went for the marble and found Lucy-Anne's hand. He felt her fingers, her thumb and her wrist.

"Hey, that tickles!"

"I'm just checking you're not fooling me," he said, letting go.

"Well, now you know I'm not, what are you going to do?"

Daddy said he supposed he'd have to take her to the doctor. When Lucy-Anne said she wasn't ill, he said, "I don't know what you are, Lucy-Anne, but the doctor might."

A puzzled dog followed them down their street when they set off, ten minutes later, and a lady with a shopping basket on wheels would have run over Lucy-Anne if Lucy-Anne hadn't skipped out of the way.

In the next street, she found a small rubber ball on the ground. She picked it up. An old man with a walking-stick stopped and watched in some alarm as the ball came bouncing along the pavement.

"Look at that! Just look at that!" he shouted, waving his stick in the air.

Lucy-Anne gave the ball to her daddy to hold so the man would calm down.

When they arrived at the doctor's, they went first of all to the secretary's office. The secretary didn't seem surprised to hear that Lucy-Anne was invisible.

"When you've worked at the doctor's as long as I have," she said, "you've seen all there is to be seen."

"But I'm not to be seen," said Lucy-Anne.

Daddy said, "Manners."

The secretary got out Lucy-Anne's medical records and told the two of them to wait in the waiting-room.

The waiting-room was large, with posters on the walls, chairs round the edge and a magazine table in the middle. Sitting on the chairs were: a woman with a boy with a bump on his forehead, a small old woman and a small old man, a woman with a baby, a man with a hankie, and a runner wearing training shoes and shorts.

"Excuse my cold," said the man with the hankie.

"I should be out jogging," said the runner. "But I tripped on a sticking up paving-stone. Look at the bruise on my knee."

Everyone looked and made concerned noises.

"Not as bad as the bump on my head," said the boy.

"Mine hurts more," said the runner.

"*You* don't look ill," said the boy to Daddy.

"Manners," said his mother, and Lucy-Anne knew how it felt to be told that, when all you'd said was something that was true.

"Well, I'm not ill," said Daddy. "It's my daughter."

"And I'm not ill, either," said Lucy-Anne, "just invisible."

"I had that," said the small old man, "in 1947."

"If nothing else works," said the tall man to Daddy, "you could try a coat of paint."

Lucy-Anne didn't think much of that suggestion and might have said something really rude – but she thought the man probably had enough worries with whatever was wrong with him. Indeed, no one looked particularly happy. The woman with the baby looked as if she'd been up all night.

This whole room needs cheering up, said Lucy-Anne to herself. And the more she thought about it, the more she thought she had a duty to do it, being the only cheerful one there apart from Daddy and he was reading.

"Who wants to play a game?" she called out.

No one replied except Daddy, who said, "This isn't the right place for games, Lucy-Anne."

"Why not?" she said.

"Yes, why not?" said the small old man.

"Because I happen to be ill," said the tall man.

"And I've got a bump on my head," said the boy.

"Well, you won't get any better by moaning," said the small old man.

"True enough," said the man with the hankie.

"Start the game," said the small old woman, "and less chatter."

"Right, everyone," called Lucy-Anne,

49

"we'll play hide-and-seek. You're all the seekers. You must count to twenty slowly and then find me. I won't leave the room. Go!"

The counting began. "One, two, three, four, five..."

Where could she hide? Under the table? No, too obvious.

"Six, seven, eight, nine, ten..."

Just sit in her seat? No, far too obvious.

"Eleven, twelve, thirteen, fourteen, fifteen..."

On top of the cupboard?

"Sixteen, seventeen..."

Yes!

"Eighteen, nineteen..."

She scrambled up.

"Twenty! Ready!" they all shouted. "Coming to get you!"

They searched, bumping into each other

and clutching about. Lucy-Anne felt quite superior, up on the cupboard. She had to work hard to stop herself giggling, seeing them all with their arms held in front of them, fingers going like spiders.

The runner tried the top of the cupboard. Lucy-Anne lifted first one leg and then the other, as his two hands felt along the edge; he went away, having missed her. A little later, the woman with the baby tried the cupboard again and Lucy-Anne again did the one leg trick.

"I bet she's left the room," exclaimed the boy with the bump on his head.

"I haven't!" shouted Lucy-Anne.

They all stopped and tried to agree where the shout had come from. But the room had been noisy and the shout had been unexpected; consequently, everyone was certain about quite different places.

"Let's pile all the chairs up," suggested the runner.

And they did. They pushed them into the centre of the room so there would be nothing for Lucy-Anne to hide behind, and they could search more easily.

"I bet she's hanging from the lamp," said the man with the hankie.

"Don't be daft," said Daddy, but he tried anyway and she wasn't.

"Let's stand still," said the small old woman.

Everyone stopped and just felt around them, as high as they could reach and then low down.

"All stop," said the woman with the baby. "Now, complete quiet and let's listen!"

They all stopped and stood.

"You won't find me," whispered Lucy-Anne.

All eyes turned in the direction of the cupboard.

"There she is!" shouted the boy with the bump on his head.

And there she most certainly was – as visible as they were.

"Oh," said Lucy-Anne, a little disappointed, "I've come back."

Just then the secretary hurried into the room. "Lucy-Anne," she called, "the doctor is waiting for you."

Lucy-Anne climbed down off the cupboard. "Tell the doctor I'm all right now."

"Say thank you," said Daddy.

"Thank you," said Lucy-Anne.

The secretary looked around. "What a mess this room is!"

"We'll tidy up," said the runner.

And they did. Lucy-Anne and Daddy

"There she is!" shouted the boy with the bump on his
head.

helped out and in no time the chairs were back in their places. They tidied the magazines, too, and the room ended up better than when they had come in.

"I really enjoyed that," said the small old man.

"My headache's gone," said the tall man. "So I'll be off."

"My knee feels much better," said the runner.

And in fact the tall man and the runner went home without waiting for the doctor, which just goes to show.

The small old woman gave Lucy-Anne a kiss, the old man shook her hand, and the boy with the bump gave her some chocolate.

"Get well soon, everyone!" she called as she and Daddy walked out through the waiting-room door.

The doll's house had two floors.

LUCY-ANNE
AND THE DOLL'S HOUSE

One day Lucy-Anne was playing with her
doll's house in her bedroom. The doll's
house had two floors. On the top floor was
a family of bears. Lucy-Anne had put
mummy bear in front of an easel, painting.
She'd put the little bear in bed, and daddy
bear on a sofa watching television with a tiny
can of beer.

On the ground floor lived a man and a
woman. They were made from wool, cork
and pipe-cleaners, and they lounged on a
sofa in front of a table piled high with food.
Around them was furniture that Lucy-Anne
had made from matchboxes and old

cardboard. What a trouble she'd had with the cardboard cupboard! She hadn't been able to stop it toppling over and, in the end, had stuck it to the wall. But the paper-fasteners made excellent brass knobs on the matchbox chest of drawers.

"I wonder what it looks like to them," said Lucy-Anne, moving her head this way and that, trying to imagine what it would all be like if she were as small as the little man and woman.

"Why don't you come in and find out?" said the woman.

Lucy-Anne was a little surprised to hear her talk, as she had never done so before.

"Well, I'd like to," she said, "but I'm too big."

"Too big? Just walk in through the door!" said the man. "And do close it after you."

Lucy-Anne thought a bit, and then

stopped thinking and opened the door and went in.

She stood in the hallway, a little smaller than the bookshelves she had made out of a stock-cube box. Some of her folded-paper books had fallen over and she took the opportunity to stand them up. She decided she must do something about the hallway. It looked a bit neglected. The pipe-cleaner hatstand was bent out of shape and the grandfather clock could do with a new face. Close up, she didn't like the wallpaper either. Originally it had been flowery wrapping-paper and the flowers were enormous.

Lucy-Anne closed the front door as she'd been told and knocked on the sitting-room door.

The man answered it. It was very strange to see him full-size when she had only known him as a doll. One of his arms was fatter than the other and there was a bit of loose wool sticking out of his neck. He was lumpy in not quite the right places – but, Manners, she told herself. I'd better keep such thoughts to myself.

"Mary!" he called. "We've got a guest!"

"Oh, goody!" shouted Mary. "We haven't had a guest for ages."

"We've never, ever had one," said the man. "Do come in."

Lucy-Anne went into the sitting-room, where Mary was lying on the sofa.

"Have some food," Mary said. "We've got lots."

Lucy-Anne helped herself to some of the food on the table: a big cream cake and a jelly, which caught her eye. Of course she had put them there, but they had been tiny then. Now they were huge. They didn't look all that appetizing, but the man and the woman didn't seem to mind, so perhaps it didn't matter. Lucy-Anne watched them holding things up to their mouths as if they were eating and she did the same.

When they'd done enough eating, Mary said, "Let me show you the bathroom."

Lucy-Anne followed her through the door on the far side of the room.

The towel in the bathroom was rather grubby and the toilet seat was wonky. But none of these things that Lucy-Anne noticed seemed to bother the dolls.

When they returned to the sitting-room, Lucy-Anne asked, "Are you happy here?"

The two dolls looked at each other.

"Yes, very happy, thank you," the man said firmly.

But Mary began, "If only there wasn't the gi—" She said "gi" like "pie" with a "j".

"Stop!" said the man. "What's the use of bringing that up? What could she do to help?"

Mary looked cross but didn't say anything more.

Lucy-Anne thought they might have had a row if she hadn't been there, so she concentrated on her cake and wondered what a gi was.

After some minutes of silence, Mary leaned over and whispered in her ear, "I'll tell you something we haven't got that we'd really love – a child."

"I heard that," the man said grumpily.

"Well, you've said so yourself," said Mary, "and where's the harm in mentioning it now?"

"Wouldn't it be a bit crowded?" Lucy-Anne asked. "Where would a child sleep?"

"She could sleep in the sink," said the

man. "There's no water in it. We never wash anything."

"I don't think that would be right, George," said Mary. "A bed would be more suitable."

"Oh, yes, a bed!" said Lucy-Anne.

She looked round the room. It might be a bit of a squash but she could imagine a child's bed in here.

"Apart from that," she said (and the gi, she thought, but not out loud), "are you happy?"

"Well," began Mary, "we don't know who built this house –"

"And we'd never complain," said George, "especially with people sleeping on the streets –"

"But have you ever been anywhere with two floors and no staircase?"

Lucy-Anne said she hadn't.

63

*Lucy-Anne's thoughts were interrupted by
a booming shout.*

"We hear the people upstairs," said George.

"And we've got all this food – but we can't share it," said Mary.

"Oh dear," said Lucy-Anne.

She thought about it while she rearranged the pile of food on the table. It had happened because *she* didn't need stairs: she could reach everywhere in the doll's house by just putting in her hand.

Her thoughts were interrupted by a booming shout that shook the whole room.

"LUCY-ANNE, WHERE ARE YOU?"

Mary gave a little scream. "The giant!"

"Freeze!" hissed George.

"LUCY-ANNE, YOUR DINNER WILL GET COLD!"

Cakes and jellies tumbled to the floor.

The shout didn't come again, but the dolls were so frightened they wouldn't unfreeze.

Lucy-Anne had to say goodbye to them as they sat unmoving, with fixed, blank expressions. She thanked them for what she'd eaten and the look round their home, but they showed no sign of having heard.

Outside the doll's house, Lucy-Anne whooshed up to normal size so fast it was like going up in a lift. And as soon as she had, she went down for her dinner.

"Daddy," she said when she was sitting with him at the table, "I've been playing with my doll's house. Can we put in some stairs?"

"A bit tricky, stairs," said Daddy. "But all right, we'll have a go."

"And one other thing," Lucy-Anne went on.

"Yes?"

"Could you not shout so loudly? You sound like a gi—"

He raised his eyebrows.

"You frighten the dolls."

"Ah," he said. "Well, I'll bear it in mind."

And he did. That weekend, he made a wooden staircase and talked to Lucy-Anne as he worked, in a whisper. Lucy-Anne glued on a red felt stair-carpet and made a little girl doll.

While Daddy was installing the stairs, Lucy-Anne was installing the doll. She put her in a matchbox, and put the matchbox in with Mary and George and all the food. It was a little crowded there now, but Lucy-Anne wasn't sorry. Then she took mummy bear, daddy bear and the child bear from the top floor and put them on the stairs.

"Mary! George!" she called (quietly). "You've got guests!"

And she picked George and Mary off their sofa, ready to meet the upstairs neighbours.

Lucy-Anne stood back to look.

LUCY-ANNE
AND THE SNOWMAN

One morning, Lucy-Anne looked out of the window and saw that everything was covered with snow. It seemed to be calling, "Come out and play – I won't be here long!"

She got dressed, washed and had breakfast. Then she put on her boots, long coat, scarf, woolly hat and gloves – and went outside.

There she made the first footprints in the crisp crackly whiteness and found the pond had frozen. She threw snowballs at the next-door fence and hoped Daddy would come out so she could pelt him.

When he didn't, she made a snowman.

She started with a snowball, as large as she could make it in her hands. Then she rolled it along the ground and it picked up more and more snow. She rolled it this way and that, so it wouldn't be sausage-shaped but round. It became harder to push as it grew bigger, until at last she had to give up pushing, just in front of her swing.

Lucy-Anne filled a bucket with snow and made a snowcastle on top of the ball. That would do for a neck. She squashed it down a bit and made another ball for a head, which she put on top.

Then she wasn't quite satisfied with the overall shape, so she slapped in extra snow here and there. She flattened the neck a bit more and built out the shoulders.

Lucy-Anne put in stones for eyes and twigs to make eyebrows. The snowman's nose was a peg and his mouth she made out of orange peel. She put real buttons down the front of his body and, to finish off, she lent him her red beret and stripy scarf.

She stood back to look and felt pleased.

But the snowman gave a groan.

"Oh," he groaned, "if I wasn't so stiff, I'd sit down!"

"The ground's very cold," said Lucy-Anne.

"I dare say I'll agree," said the snowman, "when I'm as young as you."

"No one gets younger," said Lucy-Anne.

"I do," said the snowman. "Eventually." He sighed. "Oh, I just can't wait!"

Lucy-Anne found him difficult to understand. "If you're getting younger," she said, "then how old did you start off?"

"Why, nothing days old," said the snowman.

"So how old will you finish up?"

"Why, nothing days young, of course!" He seemed to find the question silly. "You wouldn't like to give my neck a rub, would you? It's frozen solid."

Lucy-Anne came behind and massaged his neck and the top of his shoulders.

"That's better," he said. "Glad I haven't got legs – they'd only ache. But I see you've a pair. Don't you find them rather a nuisance?"

"No, I find them useful."

"What for?" asked the snowman.

"For walking and running."

"I'll never get used to you young people and your new ideas!"

"There's nothing new about walking and running," said Lucy-Anne. "Why, even the Greeks and Romans had races..."

"Stop!" exclaimed the snowman. "You'll melt my brain with all these thoughts. Feel how hot I am already."

Lucy-Anne felt but thought him extremely cold.

"Old is cold," said the snowman. "Young is..." He stopped and wrinkled his clothes-peg nose. "I don't know what young is. But I dare say I'll find out. Now sing me a song."

Lucy-Anne sang "Winter Wonderland" and the snowman's head sank into his neck, which sank into his tummy, which sank to where his legs would have been if he'd had any. When she had finished, he was fast asleep.

Next morning, much of the snow had melted. The pond wasn't frozen any more and the trees were dripping.

When Lucy-Anne looked at the snowman, she saw he was half his original size. His beret had slipped down over his eyes and his clothes peg nose was coming out.

She adjusted the beret and pushed the nose in.

"Thanks for that," said the snowman. "What a beautiful morning, eh?"

"The snow is melting," said Lucy-Anne.

"Cheer up," said the snowman.

"You seem younger," she said.

"Oh, I am. In fact, I'm no longer a snowman at all."

"What are you?"

"A snowboy, of course! And soon I'll be a snowbaby."

Lucy-Anne was going to ask what he'd be after that but she didn't because she thought he wouldn't be very much at all.

"Any grown-ups about?" said the snowboy.

"Daddy's inside," said Lucy-Anne.

"Then how about a skip?"

Lucy-Anne fetched her skipping-rope. She wasn't sure how he would manage, so she just draped it round his neck. But in fact the snowboy skipped as if he'd been born to it.

"Mary Jane went to Spain
In a chocolate aeroplane.
The door fell in,
She fell out
And landed on a chimney spout!"

His rope was twirling so fast, she could barely see it. She couldn't see his legs either, but wasn't surprised when she remembered he hadn't got any. Still, each jump was beautifully done and his face beamed with pleasure.

At last he threw down the rope, did a perfect somersault and stood on his head.

"I am so young, so ever so young!" he

exclaimed, still upside down.

He sprang upright and began pelting Lucy-Anne with snowballs. Lucy-Anne threw them back, but the snowboy made them twice as fast and threw them twice as hard.

"Enough!" she shouted, and when he took no notice she left him and ran for the garden shed.

How exhausting the snowboy was! She couldn't possibly keep up with him. She brushed snow off herself and peeked out of the window.

The snowboy was twirling round the top bar of the swing like a white Catherine-wheel.

"Oh, it's a great life!" he yelled.

He cartwheeled off the bar and landed upright on the ground in front of the swing.

Lucy-Anne was about to clap but thought she'd better not draw his attention again, in case he went back to snowballing her. She just crept quietly into the house.

Next day, when she came out into the garden, nearly all the snow had gone. There was just a drift here and there, and the odd bit on the roofs. The snowboy had grown very small, almost hidden in his scarf. The beret had come off altogether. Lucy-Anne bent close to peer into his face.

"Wanna ice-cream! Snowbaby wanna ice-cream!" He bawled so loudly, it made her jump.

"I don't know that we've got any," she said.

"Waa, waa, waa!" howled the snowbaby.

"Well, I'll go in and have a look."

In the freezer Lucy-Anne found the last bit of soft-scoop vanilla. She put it in a wafer and took it outside.

"Want strawberry!" declared the snow-baby on seeing what it was.

"This is all we have," said Lucy-Anne and handed it over.

The snowbaby dashed it to the ground. "Strawberry! Strawberry! Strawberry!"

In his dreadful rage, he seemed to be going a strawberry colour himself. Lucy-Anne hid behind a tree. The snowbaby went on for a little while, then noticed no one was there and quietened down.

But when Lucy-Anne came from behind her tree, he spotted her and yelled, "Story!"

Lucy-Anne began "Little Red Riding Hood", but she hadn't got far when he started yelling again.

She tried "Jack and the Beanstalk", "The Three Little Pigs" and "Cinderella" – but none of them worked.

"I don't know what you want," she said.

"Story! Snow story! WHITE story!"

Then Lucy-Anne understood. "Once upon a time there was a girl called Snow White..."

The snowbaby smiled. He snuggled down into his scarf and was soon asleep.

Lucy-Anne tiptoed back to the house.

At breakfast next morning, she said, "I've got a riddle for you, Daddy."

"I'm listening," he said, putting down the paper.

"What gets younger as it gets older?"

Daddy thought for a while, then said, "I give up."

"I'll show you," said Lucy-Anne.

And she led him out to the garden. But when they got there – there was nothing at all to show. Not a snowman, a snowboy, nor even a baby. The snow had gone from the garden completely.

Lucy-Anne felt very sad. She walked slowly over to her swing, where her beret and scarf lay, all soggy and wet.

"There's nothing to show," she told Daddy and picked them up.

But: "What's that?" he said suddenly.

Where her beret had lain, on the ground, was a tiny, white, bell-shaped flower.

"A snowdrop! The first of the season," said Daddy. "Isn't that nice?"

Lucy-Anne got down and cupped her hands round it. She wanted to protect it from the winter wind. But then she remembered it loved the cold; it came out of the snow. She smiled.